For
Noah x

LITTLE TIGER PRESS
An imprint of Magi Publications
1 The Coda Centre, 189 Munster Road,
London SW6 6AW
www.littletigerpress.com

First published in Great Britain 2001
by Little Tiger Press, London.
This edition published 2007

Text and illustrations copyright
© Tim Warnes 2001

Can't you sleep, Dotty?

★ ★ ★

Tim Warnes

LITTLE TIGER PRESS

Dotty couldn't sleep.
It was her first night in
her new home.

She tried sleeping
upside down.

She tried
snuggling up
to Penguin.

She even
tried lying on
the floor.

AWOOOOOOOOOOooooo

But still Dotty
couldn't sleep.

Dotty's howling woke up Pip
the Mouse. "Can't you sleep, Dotty?"
he asked. "Perhaps you should try
counting the stars like I do."

But Dotty
could only count
up to one. *That*
wasn't enough to
send her to sleep.

What could she do next?

AWOOOOOOOOOO

Susie the Bird was awake now. "Can't you sleep, Dotty?" she chirped. "I always have a little drink before I go to bed."

Chirp!

Chirp!

Dotty went to her bowl
and had a little drink.

But then she made a tiny puddle. Well *that* wouldn't help! What *could* Dotty do to get to sleep?

AWOOOOOOOOO...

Whiskers the Rabbit had woken up,
too. "Can't you sleep, Dotty?" he
mumbled sleepily. "I hide in my den
at bedtime. That always works."

Dotty dived under her blanket so
that only her bottom was showing.
But it was all dark under there with
no light at all.

Boing!

Dotty was too scared to go to sleep.

Tommy the Tortoise
poked his head from
out of his shell.

"Can't you sleep, Dotty?" he sighed. "I like
to sleep where it's bright and sunny."

Plod
Plod

Dotty liked the idea . . .

and turned on her flashlight!

"Turn it off, Dotty!"
shouted all her friends.
"*We* can't get to sleep now!"

Poor Dotty was too tired to try
anything else. Then Tommy had
a great idea!

He helped Dotty into her bed.
What Dotty needed for the first
night in her new home was . . .

to snuggle among *all* her
new friends. Soon they
were all fast asleep.

Good night, Dotty.